THE WARRIOR'S ROAD

VERMOK
THE SPITEFUL
SCAVENGER

With special thanks to Gillian Philip
For William Lloyd, former Monster Hunter, and
his sister, Sophie

www.beastquest.co.uk

ORCHARD BOOKS
338 Euston Road, London NW1 3BH
Orchard Books Australia
Level 17/207 Kent St, Sydney, NSW 2000

A Paperback Original
First published in Great Britain in 2013

Beast Quest is a registered trademark of Beast Quest Limited
Series created by Beast Quest Limited, London

Text © Beast Quest Limited 2013
Cover and inside illustrations by Steve Sims © Orchard Books 2013

A CIP catalogue record for this book is available from
the British Library.

ISBN 978 1 40832 406 6

1 3 5 7 9 10 8 6 4 2

Printed in Great Britain by CPI Group (UK) Ltd, Croydon, CR0 4YY

The paper and board used in this paperback are natural recyclable
products made from wood grown in sustainable forests. The
manufacturing processes conform to the environmental regulations of
the country of origin.

Orchard Books is a division of Hachette Children's Books,
an Hachette UK company

www.hachette.co.uk

VERMOK
THE SPITEFUL
SCAVENGER

BY ADAM BLADE

ORCHARD

ICY
MOUNTAIN
REGION

ERRINEL

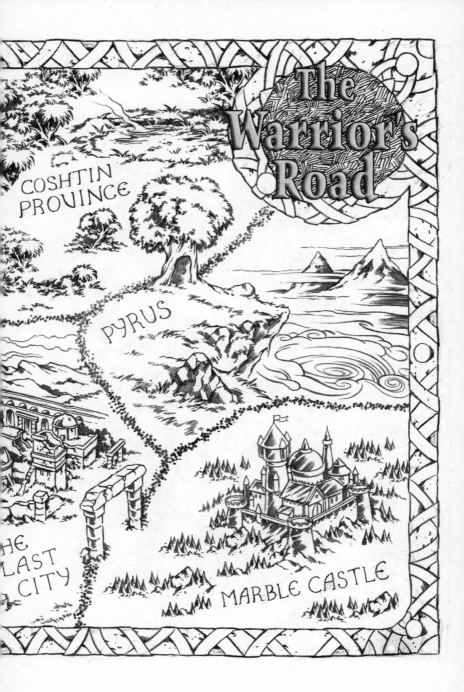

The Warrior's Road

COSHTIN PROVINCE

PYRUS

HE LAST CITY

MARBLE CASTLE

Greetings, whoever reads this.

I am Tanner, Avantia's first Master of the Beasts. I fear I have little time left. My life slips away, and I write these few words as a testament for whoever may come across my remains. I have reached the end of my final journey. But a new warrior's journey is just beginning...

With the death of a Master, a new hero must take on the responsibility of guarding the kingdom of Avantia. Avantia needs a true warrior to wear the Golden Armour. He or she must walk the Warrior's Road – a test of valour and strength. I have succeeded, but it has cost me my life. I only hope those who follow survive.

May fortune be with you,

Tanner

PROLOGUE

A black shadow flickered in the alley between two crumbled houses in the ruins of the Last City.

Is that a ghost? Uther thought, his skin prickling. But he shook himself as the shape fluttered again. Now he could see that it was nothing but a blowing, tattered curtain.

As the youngest of the small band of scavengers, Uther couldn't afford to look nervous. He was braver than his aunt Ingrid or Big Peter, or even his friend Edmund – and he'd prove it.

"Nervous, Peter?" he asked, nudging the older man.

Beneath the older man's bushy eyebrows, his small eyes darted to and fro with terror.

"Quiet, Uther!" growled Ingrid, turning to glare at him. "Keep your eyes open and your mouth shut."

"I can hear ghosts," muttered Peter, eyeing a black passageway.

"There are no ghosts!" snapped Ingrid. "The Last City has been empty for a hundred and fifty years. Now, follow me."

Uther started to follow his aunt, when the ground shuddered beneath their feet. Edmund gasped, while Peter jumped and gave a sharp cry. Uther flung out a hand against a wall to steady himself.

"It's nothing," he hissed. "Just a little tremor, that's all."

There hadn't been a huge earthquake in Uther's lifetime. Even so, the stories had been passed down through the generations. Stories of the first big earthquake, a long time ago – tremors that sent cracks racing up the sides of houses. All the people had deserted the city after a particularly bad shock, and since then the city had slowly turned itself over to decay. There were rumours that the land the city was built on was actually sinking.

Something in the ruins caught Uther's eye, and he bent to pick it up. A cracked porcelain jug.

"That's worthless," growled Edmund at his side. Uther ignored him, and stuffed it into his sack.

"We need to find a rich merchant's house," said Ingrid. "Plenty of people left in a hurry when the city was abandoned – they must have left valuables behind. Keep looking."

"Maybe we'll find the Hall of Heroes," said Uther. "The statues are supposed to be plated with gold!"

Ingrid laughed. "That would be quite a find. But maybe Vermok will find you first!"

Vermok's just a fairy tale to scare naughty children! Uther thought. He knew there was no such thing as the Spiteful Scavenger.

Another shadow scuttled past Uther's feet, and he gasped in alarm. But it was only a rat. Uther watched it scurry out of sight down a ragged hole up ahead.

Strange, Uther thought, wondering

how this rat could survive in an abandoned city. *If there are no people, there's no food for rats to scavenge…*

He was walking toward the crevasse when a huge shadow passed over him.

Uther froze, his heart pounding.

"Did you see that?" he asked, his voice high with fright.

"What?" said Ingrid.

"Something between the ruins," he gasped. "I felt its shadow!"

"You're a bundle of nerves," grinned Peter, delightedly. *He's glad to see me rattled*, Uther thought.

"Shadows are scary, aren't they, Uther?" Edmund said, joining in with the teasing. "Too many scary stories, Uth— *Aaahhhh!*"

Two thick cords lashed out of the darkness, wrapping round Edmund's ankles and dragging him towards the ruins. He was still screaming as Uther raced after him, his body being hauled over fallen rubble, his face white as he screamed in terror.

But before Uther could catch up, Edmund vanished, yanked around a corner.

Uther sprinted after him, stumbling on piles of rubble. He turned the corner – and came to a dead stop, his heart pounding in his chest.

Before him was a giant, hairless rat-like creature, with huge spikes running the length of its bulging back. Two vicious tusks jutted from its glistening nostrils. Frozen with terror, Uther stared into orange eyes that burned with evil.

A desperate cry jolted him from his trance. Edmund was beneath the

monster, struggling to free his legs
from its two scaly tails. Revolting
drool spattered him as the monstrous
rat reared up.

Desperately, Uther looked round
for Peter and Ingrid, but they were
nowhere in sight – all he could hear
was their running, fading footsteps.
The cowards! Uther picked up
Edmund's dropped sack, and hurled it
at the Beast.

It smacked into the rat's eyes, and it
gave a squealing hiss of fury. Finally
Edmund jerked the clinging tails from
his ankles and staggered clear, fleeing
back the way they'd come.

Uther tried to duck and flee after
Edmund, but the Beast's jaws sprayed
his face with saliva. Reeling sideways,
Uther crashed against a wall.

At that instant, the earth heaved
and shook. Uther felt the ground
tilt violently beneath him. The wall
swayed, then toppled. The last thing
he heard was the enraged screams of

the monster, and the rumbling crash of masonry.

Then Uther's vision, and the world, went black.

CHAPTER ONE

CITY OF GHOSTS

This portal was a deadly trick!

Horror flooded Tom – he was plunging through the sky towards the ground. He tried to cry a warning to Elenna, but the words were flung back in his throat. Helpless, he twisted through the air. Above him, he saw Elenna and her wolf, Silver, tumbling from the portal in the sky.

Cold air rushed past him as the

ground raced up towards him with terrifying speed. *I'm going to die – I've led Elenna to her death!* Shutting his eyes, he braced himself for the collision, for his bones to shatter and his heart to stop.

But I'm still falling...

Tom blinked his eyes open again. The air still rushed into his face, and he was still spinning and tumbling... but not so fast. He was falling through a layer of puffy white clouds which seemed to cling like damp hands, cushioning his fall. Tom saw Silver and then Elenna hit the cloud layer – and they too were buffeted as they fell.

Elenna was wide-eyed and silent, but Silver was howling in confusion, his legs flailing as he plunged softly into another cloud. Then, abruptly, the cloud around Tom frayed and dissolved, and his feet touched the ground with a gentle jolt.

The last of the cloud drifted away, and Tom gasped as he gazed at the gigantic, crumbling archway before him.

The sky was clear and golden now, with only a few last flecks of cloud. Beyond the arch lay a sprawling city that looked proud and beautiful in the soft sunshine. But it took Tom only moments to realise that it was a trick of the light. What had once been a great city was now wrecked and broken. At the crest of the archway were chipped and weathered letters, warning:

BRAVES OR FOOLS, WALK THIS WAY.

Swallowing hard, Tom turned to

watch Elenna and Silver land behind him. The wolf gave a scared yelp as he rolled, then leaped back onto all fours.

Elenna ran to Tom's side. Already she held her bow ready, though her fingers trembled slightly. Together they gazed at the empty city beyond the archway. Not a single figure moved in the ruined streets. "Where are we?" she asked, breathless.

Tom shook his head. "I don't know. A long way from Avantia, that's for sure."

"I wonder what happened here?" Elenna took a cautious step closer. "It must have been a beautiful city once. Look at those gilded domes – and that aqueduct!"

Sure enough, Tom saw a raised waterway on massive arches stretched

across much of the city – like
everything else he could see, it was
broken and crumbling. *The city must
have housed thousands of people once*, he
thought.

"There must have been a disaster,"
Tom murmured. "Look at the cracks

in that wall – and the holes in the ground. I wonder if there's anyone left alive."

"Perhaps we'll find out – if the Warrior's Road leads through the city?" said Elenna. At her side Silver whined doubtfully, and she stroked his thick mane.

Tom reached into his tunic, pulling out his Stoneglass fragment. Ever since he'd lost his magical map, his ability to see the Warrior's Road had become less and less reliable. He was grateful to the young witch, Petra, for giving him this chunk of crystal.

Raising it to his eye, he saw the red glow of the cobblestones. Sure enough, the Road led beneath the archway and along the marble-paved avenue beyond.

"I can see it," said Tom. He pointed

at the ominous words above the arch. "So whether I'm brave or foolish, I must walk this way."

"Be careful," warned Elenna. "This place looks dangerous."

Tom nodded. Walking the Warrior's Road had been outlawed for centuries, until the evil Judge had stripped Tom of his Golden Armour and its powers. Making this perilous journey was now the only way that he could win back his status as Avantia's Master of the Beasts. If Tom did not defeat the six fearsome Beasts who guarded the Road, Avantia would lose its only protector against evil.

But no one had survived the Road in two hundred years. Many valiant young men and women had died making the attempt.

Tom gritted his teeth. "While there's blood in my veins, I won't turn back. We've come too far to let the Judge beat us now."

They set off into the ruined city, Silver pacing between them with his

hackles raised. There was no sign of survivors. The citizens must have left in a great hurry. Doors and windows stood open, hanging from their hinges, and walls had been smashed to rubble. Some of the buildings had collapsed altogether, and the water trickling through the ditches was green and stinking.

"I wonder if – oh!" Elenna's words were cut off as the ground gave a sudden heave beneath their feet. Tom's heart pounded as he fought to keep his balance. In the distance, there was a roar like thunder as a tower shuddered, then collapsed.

Then, as quickly as it had begun, the tremor subsided.

"An earthquake." Elenna took a breath. "That must have been what destroyed this city."

"It looks like it," agreed Tom as aftershocks rippled around them. "Watch out!" He pulled Elenna sideways just as a stone lion on top of a column teetered, then crashed to the ground.

Silver growled nervously, his coat bristling. Elenna laid her hand on his head to soothe him, and he fell silent, sniffing the air. Then, with a sharp growl, he bounded into a ruined alley.

"Silver! What's there?" Elenna followed her wolf, climbing nimbly over rubble.

Tom paused, his fingers curled round his sword-hilt. There might be any number of dangers here, and not just from earthquakes. *How many before me ever reached this city?* he wondered. *And how many survived to go further on the Warrior's Road?*

He had already conquered four Beasts on this Quest, but each battle had been harder than the one before. At least each defeated Beast left Tom a token he was able to use on the next Quest. Linka had left him a single tawny feather and it was stored inside his tunic. *When the time is right, I'll know how to use it*, he thought.

Even so, a horrible feeling of doubt settled in his stomach as he remembered the mysterious man they had met when Tom fought Linka, the Sky Conqueror. *What if the Hooded Man was right…? What if this is the one Quest I can't complete?*

CHAPTER TWO

ATTACKED

Tom's anxious thoughts were interrupted by a cry from Elenna.

"Silver's found something," she shouted. "It's a body!"

Hope burned inside Tom as he followed Elenna across the piles of broken stone. *So there may be survivors after all!* But as he crouched at her side in the alley, his heart sank.

Silver was sniffing at a great heap

of rubble, but all that was visible was a booted foot, sticking out at an awkward angle. The stones were huge, and the foot wasn't moving. Whoever had been buried by this falling wall, there was no hope for him. Touching the limp ankle gently, Tom felt sickened. The flesh was still warm beneath his fingertips.

"This man died not long ago," he said. "I should have been quicker, Elenna. I could have got here in time to..."

Elenna laid a hand on his shoulder. "You can't save everyone," she said.

All the same...if I'd faced my challenges better, got here sooner... Shaking his head, Tom dragged his eyes away from the body. Nearby lay a sack. *That must have belonged to this poor man...*

Tom picked it up and rummaged

inside. He blinked in surprise as he
pulled out its contents. "Nothing but
a cracked old jug. What was he doing
here, I wonder?"

Elenna took the pitcher from him.
"Who knows? But he must have been
caught out by a quake."

A small shadow scuttled at the edge

of Tom's vision. He saw a glimpse of a long, greasy tail. "Rats!" he said, shooing the creature away with his foot. "Pass me some more stones, Elenna. If we can't give this man a proper burial, we can at least keep the scavengers away."

Elenna picked up fallen stones and passed them to Tom, who piled them over the exposed foot. As he stepped back, dusting his hands, another rat ran across the makeshift grave-covering. It was joined by another – and then a third.

One sniffed and rose up on its hind legs, but when Tom kicked out at it, it ran only a short distance, then glared at him and sneaked closer.

"They're not even frightened of us," said Elenna, tossing a chunk of brick in its direction. "Go away!"

Tom glanced around. More rats scurried behind him. Silver snapped and growled, but each time they managed to drive the creatures back a little, more scampered from their holes. There was a sudden wriggling movement behind Elenna and she leaped forwards as an ugly dark shape scrabbled up the back of her tunic.

"Ah!" Elenna screamed and slapped at her neck, knocking away the big black rat. "It bit me!"

Silver caught the rat up in his teeth and flung it away, but more and more were flocking towards them, undeterred by the wolf's jaws or Tom's flailing sword. *We've faced so many Beasts*, Tom thought. *But this is nearly as disgusting!* He felt sick to his stomach as the rats clambered over each other, teeth bared and whiskers twitching, desperate to attack. *Have they been driven mad by hunger?*

"Let's climb away from them," said Tom, swiping a rat from his leg with a shudder. "Come on!"

They ran to over to a crumbling wall to their right and began to climb. The stones felt loose and treacherous beneath their hands and feet, but scrambling up the unsafe walls still felt better than staying among the hordes of squealing vermin. Elenna was panting with fright and Tom's heart was in his throat as they finally crested the narrow wall.

"Run!" said Tom.

They ran as lightly as they could along the top of the wall. It was hardly wider than Tom's foot and he had to hold out his arms to balance his body. When they came to a sloping roof,

they kneeled to crawl up the clay tiles.
One of the tiles came loose and fell to
the ground, smashing in an explosion
of splinters. As Tom looked back, he
saw the rats swarming up in pursuit.
They were right behind them!

"We can't get rid of the brutes!"
exclaimed Elenna. "They're worse than
a Beast!"

"There!" Tom spotted a gap ahead

in the crumbling roofs. He leaped forward and landed in a shaky crouch on a broad wall on the other side. "Jump, Elenna!" He could only hope her bravery would overcome her fear of heights.

His friend sprang across the gap and began to slide on the loose stones, but Tom grabbed her arm and tugged her to safety. Silver landed too, sure-footed as ever, his tongue lolling. A rat clung to his shoulder, but he snatched it in his jaws, tossing it into the yawning chasm between the buildings.

Elenna gasped for breath. "We've lost them for now," she said.

"Let's keep going, then." Tom felt another small rumble beneath his feet. "If a bigger earthquake hits, I don't want to be up here!"

"Good point," agreed Elenna. "Look

over there, Tom – part of the wall's collapsed. That's where we can get down."

Carefully they slithered down the sloping tumble of stone, and Tom heard Elenna breathe a sigh of relief when their feet were back on solid ground.

"The next Beast might be lurking in these ruins," she said, fingering her bow.

Tom nodded. "The sooner I find it and defeat it, the sooner we can be out of this city."

The three companions moved on, treading cautiously over shattered rubble. Tom scanned the shadows for movement. The many arches and corners gave the next Beast plenty of hiding places.

"Look out," said Tom. A crack

yawned at his feet, and he held out an arm to stop Elenna.

The gash in the earth was so wide, they had to make another perilous run-and-jump. Tom led the way, followed by Silver, and finally Elenna.

"We made it," Elenna gasped with relief. "But we'd better watch our feet from now on."

Tom realised they had drawn much closer to the stone aqueduct, its channel out of sight up on great arches. They were close enough now that he could make out the cracks in the structure, where discoloured water streamed down and stained the white stone. In the shadow of a high wall, they stopped and stared up. The leaking water was flecked with dirty foam. Tom could see a dead mouse caught at the edge of the parapet.

"The city's water supply," said Tom. "It's no use now – the water's poisoned. No wonder there's no one left—"

Tom fell quiet, holding his breath. He was sure he had heard a soft sound...

"It sounds like footsteps." Elenna's voice was hushed and strained.

Tom drew his sword silently from its scabbard. Listening, he heard it again – the scuffling tread of quiet feet. *Someone who doesn't want to be seen...*

A stone rolled on the wall above them, but Tom was not quick enough. A cloaked figure dropped lightly down, his blade flashing brightly in the glare of the sun – and levelled right at Tom's throat.

CHAPTER THREE

A FATEFUL MEETING

"How nice to see you again." The voice was a mocking drawl as the Hooded Man held his blade to Tom's chin.

"Save the pleasantries," spat Tom, keeping his own sword pointed at his enemy. "How did you get here?"

The Hooded Man chuckled. "The same way you did – on the Warrior's Road."

"That's impossible!" shouted Elenna.

Tom saw that her bow was already drawn, an arrow nocked on the string.

"Not possible?" sneered the man. "I've been travelling the Warrior's Road for a long time, girl. I know short cuts you can't imagine. Ones you don't want to imagine."

Tom kept his eyes on the Hooded Man's. "Who are you?" he growled.

The man only gave a chilling laugh. He raised a gloved hand to his hood, and tossed it back.

For an instant Tom's throat tightened, and he felt his heart pound painfully. *Father?*

He shook his head. *My father died!*

The keen blue eyes could have been Taladon's, and the golden beard was just like Tom's father's. But the Hooded Man's face was harder and more cruel than Taladon's had ever been. There

was a deep scar running from his ear to his lip. A bump on his nose showed it had been broken, and poorly healed.

"What?" mocked the man. "You don't recognise me?"

Slowly Tom shook his head. "Are you saying we've met before?"

The man gave a bitter laugh. "You

could say that."

But Tom felt nothing but confusion. A low growl from Silver reminded him that Elenna was there, covering him.

"Well," drawled the man, glancing at Elenna, "it is nice to see old friends."

"You're no friend of ours," snarled Elenna. She took a sideways step, crossing a narrow crevice but never taking her eyes off the Hooded Man.

"She's right," said Tom. "Why are you following us?"

The Hooded Man sighed. "I'd talk better without a sword in my face."

"I could say the same," said Tom. "And I don't trust you not to—"

A violent force flung Tom sideways. The Hooded Man staggered too, thrown off balance, and Elenna gave a yell of shock. *Another quake?* As Silver crouched, whining, Tom half fell.

The Hooded Man was first to recover, rebalancing and wielding his blade deftly. A jerk of his wrist and Tom's sword flew from his grasp and into the air. His enemy caught it by the hilt. *No!*

Tom heard the hiss of an arrow past his ear. The Hooded Man dropped his own sword, its clatter almost drowned out by the growing roar of the quake. He clutched his hand, and Tom saw blood between his fingers.

"Got you!" exclaimed Elenna triumphantly, seizing a second arrow.

The Hooded Man gave a shout of rage as he charged at Elenna, giving her a fierce shove that sent her tumbling backwards towards a wide crevasse.

Tom dashed forward, but his fist closed on thin air. Elenna toppled backwards, and fell with a cry into the blackness of the chasm.

CHAPTER FOUR

INTO THE DEPTHS

"No!" Horrified, Tom raced to the edge of the chasm. "Elenna!" he yelled.

"Elenna...lenna...lenna..." All that answered him was an echo, and Tom felt a surge of despair. With a yelp, Silver came to his side and pressed himself against Tom's legs.

Then, faintly, he heard a weak voice. "I'm all right."

Tom's head spun with relief, and he

blew out a sigh, closing his eyes briefly. He heard the retreating footsteps of the Hooded Man making his escape, but his enemy could wait. Right now he had his friend to worry about – and after that, the Beast Quest.

"Are you injured?" Tom called down.

Elenna's voice drifted back up. "I've twisted my ankle."

"Don't try to move." Tom turned to the anxious Silver, stroking his muzzle, then lifted the Hooded Man's sword. It was heavy, with a crude leather-bound hilt, and a blade that was nicked and scratched. Tom felt a wrench of regret at the loss of his own weapon – but this one would have to do for now. He pushed it into his belt.

"Wait here," he told the wolf. "I'll bring Elenna back."

Silver yipped, and Tom felt his yellow

eyes fixed on him as he lowered himself into the crevasse. *There are handholds – if I take it carefully, I can get down. But if Elenna's hurt, how will I bring her back up?*

There was no time to worry about that. The jagged crack of sky above him grew smaller and smaller as Tom climbed down, feeling for the fragile hand and footholds that took him ever deeper into the darkness. Tom looked up. The daylight above him was only a thin line, now that he was so far down.

There was just enough dim light to show him that he was standing in a tunnel. From the hacked scars of axes on the walls it seemed man-made, and sluggish water trickled muddily along the ground.

It's a sewer, Tom guessed, wrinkling his nose at the smell.

"Tom." Elenna was propped against a

wall. Her forehead was bleeding and her clothes were torn, but she gave him a rueful smile. "Sorry I was clumsy."

"Don't be silly." He smiled back, despite his rising anxiety. Tearing a strip of fabric from his tunic, he began to bind up her ankle. "I wish I could use Epos's

magic talon to help this heal, but..."

"But the Judge would accuse you of cheating," finished Elenna. "Don't give him an excuse, Tom. I'll be fine." As he drew back, she got shakily to her feet and said, "See? It's not too bad."

From the strain on her face, Tom knew that his friend was only being brave. *She certainly won't be able to scramble out of here...*

"Come on," he said, steadying her. "Let's see if we can find a way out through these tunnels. There's no way you can climb back up that sheer drop."

As Tom glanced around the tunnel, his heart sank. He could see several black passageways leading from this one, some twisting upwards, some plunging into deeper darkness.

Taking a deep breath, he chose one of the rising tunnels and set off, letting

Elenna lean against him. But they hadn't gone far when the tunnel dipped again, and twisted. At the next turn, the tunnel branched in two.

Where to now? Tom turned to the left fork, but hesitated. "If this is wrong, we'll have to retrace our steps. And the tunnel will branch again – I'd stake my Golden Armour on it. We could get lost down here forever."

"Mark the way we've come," suggested Elenna. "Scratch a sign on the wall of the tunnel we choose."

"Good idea," said Tom. Pulling the Hooded Man's sword from his belt, he scored a deep mark on the tunnel wall. "Let's hope we've picked the exit first time," he told Elenna cheerfully. "Then we won't need the marks."

But as they pressed on through the maze of tunnels, Tom found himself scratching more and more signs at the endless branching turns. Now and again a blast of air told Tom there were shafts above them, but they were too sheer for Elenna to climb.

"That's a lot like your own sword," remarked Elenna as dim light from an air shaft caught the blade. "Are you sure you've never seen the Hooded Man before? He looked just like your father."

Tom shook his head. "I'm certain. Taladon would never have such a cruel sneer! Whatever the Hooded Man is up to, he's playing games with us." *Where is the Hooded Man now?* Tom wondered. *He could be anywhere, spreading trouble.*

"Look!" Elenna suddenly cried. "There's proper light ahead."

She was right – but the light they could see was not welcoming daylight. It was the flickering, reddish glow of…

"Flames!" he said.

They flattened themselves against the tunnel wall as shadows appeared, moving towards them. Tom felt Elenna tremble beside him. He held his breath as three figures emerged from the gloom.

People! The thin, bedraggled figures gripped torches. Two were men, and the one in the lead was a woman. All of them glanced constantly over their shoulders. *They look scared...*

Tom stepped out into their path, sword in hand. They jumped and flinched back, the younger man giving a cry of shock.

The woman brandished her torch defensively. "Who are you?" she cried.

Tom lowered his weapon. "My name is Tom. My friend Elenna here fell into the tunnels and got trapped, and we're finding our way out."

The woman eyed him nervously for a

few seconds, then nodded. "I'm Ingrid.
I came to the city with Peter and young
Edmund here. And my nephew Uther.
But he was lost…" Her voice faltered
and Edmund gave a choked sob.

"Uther was my friend," Edmund said,
his eyes filled with grief. "He saved my
life when the Beast attacked us both.

But he was crushed by a falling wall."

Grimly, Tom exchanged glances with Elenna, who nodded sadly. *The foot we found emerging from the rubble...*

"You two are a curious pair," Ingrid interrupted. "You say you're trapped down here, but what are you doing in the city at all?"

"We..." Tom thought desperately. "We were travelling through—"

"You're a warrior!" exclaimed Edmund as his eyes lit on Tom's sword. "You were walking the Warrior's Road!"

"Don't be a fool, boy," snapped Ingrid. "That's a legend, nothing more."

"You didn't believe in Vermok, either," retorted Edmund. "Until he attacked us."

The Beast! Tom glanced from one to the other. "What do you mean?"

"They say this place was on the route of an ancient journey for heroes,"

Edmund told him. "That's why the city was built here. It housed a grand chamber, a room full of statues of—"

"*Aieeee!*"

A strangled scream cut off Edmund's words. Tom turned toward where Peter had stood and gasped. A leathery rope had coiled round the man's throat and was yanking him upwards!

Tom leaped up, but Peter was already out of reach. The man kicked and gasped, hauling desperately at the cord round his neck.

"We'll help!" Tom cried. They ran to grab Peter's ankles, but Tom's hands only found thin air as the rope pulled the older man higher and higher.

It's taking him, Tom thought. *I have to do something!*

But with a last hoarse shriek, Peter vanished into a black shaft.

CHAPTER FIVE

THE SPITEFUL SCAVENGER

"The Beast has taken Peter, too!" Ingrid wailed.

Something tumbled from the dark shaft: Peter's torch, the flame extinguished. A tendril of smoke curled from it, then faded.

Stunned and angry, Tom turned to Ingrid. "This Beast – can you describe it?" he said.

The woman was pale, her limbs trembling. She pointed at Edmund. "He's the only one who saw it clearly."

"It's like a rat," said Edmund, his voice shaking. "But much bigger… It's three times as big as a horse. Its skin is bald, like leather. It has tusks, and its teeth…" He glanced up fearfully. "They're big enough to tear a person apart."

Tom stepped forward. He held the Hooded Man's sword in one hand, extending the other for Ingrid's torch. She passed it to him silently.

Brandishing the flame, Tom shouted up into the shaft, his voice clear and challenging. "Vermok! I am Tom of Avantia – and I've come to defeat you!"

His voice echoed eerily through the endless rocky tunnels.

Darkness seemed to close in tighter around them, and the silence was agonisingly long. At last it was broken by the sound of scratching, padding feet and snuffling breaths. Tom's torch flared, throwing a shadow against the far wall of the cavern – a shadow that grew larger, and larger still. Tom lifted his sword. At his side, Elenna drew and nocked an arrow.

The shadow shrank, then vanished.

"It's afraid," Edmund whispered, sounding hopeful.

"No," said Tom firmly, shaking his head. "It's just toying with us."

A vile smell drifted to his nostrils, one that caught in his throat and almost made him gag. He heard a phlegmy, snuffling noise as the Beast got closer.

Where are you? Tom's eyes darted

around at the cavern shadows as Elenna turned a slow circle.

A foul stench touched his nostrils, and he spun round and looked up. The flame lit up a high slanting tunnel, but it was too late. A huge shape barrelled out of the shaft above, slamming into Tom. He did not have time to defend himself. He was lifted up on two curved tusks and flung through the dank air.

Tom's shoulder exploded with pain as he crashed against the cavern wall so hard that his breath was knocked from his lungs. In a daze, he saw the others scrambling away in a panic. The Beast was above him, rearing and turning, its fiery eyes blazing.

Tom flung up his shield to block the creature's next strike. *How long can I hold it off?* he thought desperately.

Then he heard Elenna's
commanding voice. "Vermok!"

*She didn't run with the others – but
she's injured!* Lowering his shield, Tom
began to shout a warning – only to
hear the soft hiss of an arrow.

Vermok squealed, wriggled round
and fled, a feathered shaft stuck in his

flank. The last Tom saw of the giant rat was its two long tails like snapping behind it like a whipcord, before it squirmed into a tunnel and vanished.

Panting and aching from the attack, Tom clambered to his feet. *This Beast is cunning*, he thought. *It knows how to lurk in the shadows, and ambush when it's least expected. Well, I won't give it the chance to do that again!*

"Stay here, Elenna!" Tom snatched up his dropped torch, adjusted his grip on his sword, and raced after the Beast.

The flames of his torch lit up the tunnels in dancing orange light. There were more branching forks, more dips and rises in the passageway. Tom might have lost Vermok's trail had it not been for the stench. That was easy enough to follow, as were the splashes of glutinous blood from the wound Elenna had given the Beast. Tom ran, splashing through filthy water, hearing the grunts of the monster not far ahead. He sprinted round a bend in the tunnel, then halted.

The cavern stretched ahead, empty – but something caught Tom's eye on the stone floor: the broken shaft of Elenna's arrow. The Beast had to have turned sharply to break the shaft...

There's a side tunnel, he realised. Searching the shadows, he felt a blast of cold air. *There it is!* He ran into the tunnel, giving chase to the Beast.

Vermok's stench was even more powerful in such narrow confines. Tom broke into a run, his breath coming harder and faster as he pounded uphill. A blast of light suddenly dazzled him. There was a

yawning hole ahead, surrounded
by smashed stone and the shattered
remains of a large iron grille. With
a tremor of dread, he realised that
Vermok had escaped to the surface!

Bursting out into the open air,
Tom flung away his torch. He
felt a tightness around his belly –
something had coiled tightly round
him.

It was a huge, greasy tail.

"Vermok!" yelled Tom. Flung
backwards, he was able to see the
Beast properly for the first time.

Vermok's backbone was ridged
with spikes, and its hide looked
as tough as armour, though it was
hacked about with ancient scars. This
Beast has seen a battle or ten, Tom
realised. Two yellowing tusks jutted
from its nostrils, and as Vermok's

mouth opened, Tom saw jagged fangs dripping with slime and the tattered remains of food and flesh.

The tail tightened round his body, and Tom was yanked towards the slavering jaws.

CHAPTER SIX

COMBAT IN THE CITY

Tom's left arm was pinned against his
side, but his sword arm was still free.
He raised the blade to strike – only
to feel the Beast's second tail wrap
around his wrist. Now he was helpless.
Tom dug his heels into the ground, but
the stones were loose and cracked, and
Vermok was too strong. He dragged
Tom forward, teeth snapping hungrily.

A sudden exhaustion swept through Tom. The Hooded Man's sword was loose in his grasp, and the Beast's other tail was squeezing the air from his body as a terrible thought drifted through his mind: *Is this it? Have I fought my last battle?*

His vision was blurred, and he could barely think for the pain – but he caught a flash of grey as something leaped towards him.

Silver!

The wolf's jaws snapped round Vermok's tail. Vermok gave an agonised squeal, and one of his tails loosened, freeing Tom's sword arm. Striking out, Tom's arm juddered as the blade smashed into one of the Beast's tusks. Shards of bone flew as Vermok lurched sideways, releasing Tom as he smashed against a wall.

Then he scrabbled and righted himself,
and bounded away, dragging his two
tails in a smear of blood.

Through a daze, Tom heard voices
and running feet. Whirling around, all
his muscles burning with pain, he saw
the others stumbling out of the tunnel
behind him. Ingrid and Edmund were

sharing the lead, with Elenna limping painfully behind.

"Are you all right?" shouted Elenna.

"Thanks to Silver." Tom rubbed the wolf's head gratefully. His wrist was badly bruised where Vermok's tail had squeezed it, and his ribs hurt with every breath, but it could have been worse. Elenna's wolf had saved his life.

"We should get out of the city now," said Edmund, his eyes darting in fear. "The monster could come back at any moment."

Getting his breath back, Tom drew out the precious Stoneglass and brought it to his eye, seeing the red gleam of the Warrior's Road leading further into the city. He shook his head and put a hand on Edmund's shoulder.

"You and Ingrid should go," he told him, "but Elenna and I have a path to follow. And while there's blood in my veins, that's the way I will walk. Goodbye, both of you, and stay safe!"

He and Elenna watched the other two until they disappeared round a corner, turning to wave farewell. Then Tom took a deep breath, gripping the hilt of his borrowed weapon. *If only it was my own sword...* "Let's go."

Elenna could only walk slowly, but with Tom supporting her, they made fair progress. The recent tremors had brought more buildings crashing down. Tom dodged as an ornately carved pedestal toppled, sending up clouds of dust that blinded them both and set them coughing violently.

"Is this wise?" Elenna asked, between coughs. Her short, spiked hair was thick with dust.

"It's all we can do," Tom said, as they

skirted a collapsing wall. Two more
rats ran out and they had to jump over
them. "I have to follow this Road, or
all of Avantia will be in danger."

Tom scanned the ground for his
sword, and watched every corner for a
sign of the Beast or the Hooded Man.
Two enemies were abroad, and one of
them might have Tom's own weapon.
Still, the Warrior's Road led them
straight into the depths of the city.

At the end of an alley, Tom stopped.
A vast city square lay before them.
Instead of piles of rubble, dead grass
and a cracked waterless fountain were
all that lay between them and a grand,
pillared temple. There was nowhere
to hide – Tom and Elenna would be
almost defenceless if they stepped
into the square. But Tom lifted the
Stoneglass fragment, and saw that

the Warrior's Road led directly to the temple's door.

"That's where we have to go," he murmured.

Elenna nodded, panting. "Be careful. You don't know where Vermok will be waiting."

Keeping his eyes open and his sword ready, Tom led the way across the square. Up close he could see that the temple's magnificent walls were cracked, the pillars leaning dangerously. There was a low creaking sound, as if were a struggle for the building to stand.

How long before it falls? Tom wondered.

Massive iron-studded doors hung uselessly from their hinges, and there were great dents and splinters in the wood – as if something huge had battered its way into the building. And there, on the dusty steps, were freshly scraped claw-prints.

"This way," said Tom quietly. "Hold back, keep Silver beside you, and have your bow held ready. With your bad ankle, you mustn't get too close to the Beast."

"I know," muttered Elenna under her breath. "But I'll be right behind you, Tom. You can rely on me."

Tom had barely touched the great broken door when noise exploded on the city air. It was the scream of an enraged Beast – and below that, the angry shouts of a man.

Tom sprinted inside the great temple. It took several moments for his eyes to adjust to the dimness, but at last he made out huge marble columns. The smashed pieces of old statues lay between them. A few lucky statues stood whole, or leaned where they had fallen against the pillars.

In the centre of the hall, Vermok crouched, whipping his vicious tails, snapping and tearing with his teeth and claws. Before him a man stood, slashing at the Beast with Tom's sword.

The Hooded Man!

CHAPTER SEVEN

THE EARTH SHAKES

Tom hesitated, his heart in his throat. The Hooded Man leapt across the broken tiles, darting nimbly away from Vermok's savage teeth and lashing tails, parrying the Beast's blows and returning them with powerful strikes of Tom's blade.

Vermok lunged, and the Hooded Man ducked aside and hacked at

the Beast's flank. Thick black blood
spurted from the new wound in
Vermok's hide – but he did not slow
down. The Spiteful Scavenger stalked
forward with a triumphant look in his
eyes, backing the Hooded Man steadily
into a corner.

But then the stranger sprang up onto a fallen pillar, dropping behind it and out of the Beast's lumbering reach. Despite his strength, Vermok seemed slow and clumsy.

This could still end badly, Tom warned himself. The Beast's attacks were so violent and uncontrolled as he slammed into walls and pillars, Tom feared the whole temple would come crumbling down at any moment.

He called back to Elenna and Silver at the doorway. "Keep back!"

"Tom!" Elenna shouted in warning. "You should get out, too!"

"I can't leave the Hooded Man." Tom's opponent might have been crafty and treacherous, but he would not allow him to be crushed to death! No one deserved that.

Tom ran further into the temple,

while Elenna fired arrow after arrow to cover him. Ahead, the Hooded Man was poised to strike again at Vermok's shoulder.

"You have to get out of here!" Tom shouted.

The man glanced briefly over his shoulder. "Why?"

"The building's coming down," yelled Tom. "This way, quickly!"

But with the Hooded Man's attention distracted, Vermok lashed out with one of his whip-like tails. It curled round the man's ankles, and yanked him off his feet. The Hooded Man's skull cracked against a fallen pillar.

He was out cold.

Tom gritted his teeth. *I can't let him die – no matter what he's done.*

Dodging falling stones, Tom raced

forward into the heart of the temple and struck hard at Vermok's tail. His blow was true, slicing cleanly through the leathery flesh.

Vermok screamed and flung himself sideways, colliding with another marble pillar. It toppled sideways, slamming

into the next, causing a great chunk of the roof to collapse. Tom remembered the inscription on the arch: *Braves or fools, walk this way.*

That had been no idle warning!

Tom broke into a run, dodging the statues as they fell, shattering tiles. Elenna's arrows still hissed through the air, but Vermok was no longer the biggest danger. With a thunderous crack, one of the temple walls split down the middle, spitting chunks of stone that plummeted to the ground.

Vermok was panicking now, thrashing and screeching. Catching sight of the open doors, he bounded towards them – and straight for Elenna.

"Look out!" yelled Tom, coughing as dust filled his lungs.

Elenna did not flinch. Tom saw

her calmly nock another arrow onto her bowstring and aim it at Vermok's heart. With a desperate squeal, the Beast veered around her, running for his life and disappearing back into the city streets.

My old friend's all right, thought Tom desperately. *Now I just have to save my new enemy...*

He seized the Hooded Man's armpits, trying to drag him towards the doorway. But his foe's dead weight was too much for Tom, especially after a fierce battle with a Beast.

I can't let him die, Tom thought. *What kind of Master of the Beasts would I be if I did?*

Sudden vibrations shuddered through his body, and the deafening noise that blasted his ears was like the roar of a new Beast. Looking up, Tom saw the roof give way completely. Deadly, jagged chunks of slate and tiles rained down towards him. Tom crouched, throwing his arms over himself and the Hooded Man.

This is really it, he thought. *This is the end of my Beast Quest...*

The noise faded, echoing into the sky; the ground slowly stopped shaking. Tom dared to uncover his head, opening his eyes and seeing dust rising in a cloud, beginning to settle. He blinked as he looked up. Above him and the Hooded Man lay one of the statues. It had fallen across them both, but the head had slammed into the opposite pillar and lodged there. The massive marble figure had shielded them from the collapsing roof!

Shakily, Tom climbed out from

beneath one huge marble arm, and
backed away, staring at the statue's
face, half plated in gold.

It was a face he knew – a noble face,
familiar from King Hugo's own palace.
Or rather, from the Gallery of Tombs
that lay beneath it.

"It's Tanner," Tom whispered.
"Avantia's first Master of the Beasts."

CHAPTER EIGHT

PURSUIT OF THE BEAST

"Of course it's Tanner." The Hooded Man's voice was little more than a rasping moan. Glancing down, Tom saw him trying to crawl free of the rubble.

"But I don't understand." Tom crouched down to pull the Hooded Man by one arm. "What is Tanner's statue doing here?"

"You're so clueless," mumbled his enemy. "This was once the Hall of Heroes. All who have completed the Warrior's Road are commemorated here. And you're deluded enough to think you'll join them? Hah!" He spluttered and coughed.

At a sound above them, Tom looked up. There stood Elenna, hauling a wooden beam away with Silver's help.

"Tom!" Her worried face broke into a smile, and the wolf yelped with delight. "You're alive!"

"We both are, just." Tom winked and pointed at the statue. "Tanner helped!"

Scrambling down, Elenna helped Tom drag the Hooded Man across the floor of the shattered temple and out of the vast doors into the pale sunlight. Only when they were safely at the bottom of the steps did Tom allow himself to slump back, exhausted. He and the Hooded Man were both bruised and cut, covered in stone dust. Elenna knelt to share her flask of water.

Almost grudgingly, the Hooded Man accepted a drink, then wiped his hand across his mouth. "Thank you."

"It's Tom you should thank," retorted Elenna.

"I didn't need his help." The man glowered at Tom. "I've faced Vermok several times, and I've never lost yet."

"You haven't ever beaten him, either," Tom pointed out.

The man's face darkened. "And neither will you, upstart. Your statue will never stand in the Hall of Heroes."

Maybe he's right, thought Tom grimly. *I still haven't beaten Vermok.*

Biting back his anger, Tom sheathed

his enemy's sword, and grabbed his own from the man's weakened hand. "We'll see." Glaring at him, Tom realised again how familiar the man seemed. "I've saved your life – which means, you owe me. Now tell me who you are!"

The man gave a savage laugh. "That you'll never know, Tom of Avantia."

A vicious growl echoed through the ruined streets, and they all looked up sharply. Silver's hackles bristled.

Right on top of the aqueduct squatted the Beast, its remaining tail lashing the brickwork. Small orange eyes glittered in a savage face.

"Vermok," Tom muttered. "It's time to finish this."

"But how will you reach him?" Elenna asked.

Tom frowned. One dark line on the aqueduct looked straighter than the

other cracks, and rust stained the
stonework around it. Looking closer,
Tom saw that it was an iron ladder,
built into the side of the aqueduct. He
pointed at it.

"Tom, you can't climb that!" said
Elenna. "It may not hold your weight."

"There's no other way," said Tom. "I have to face this Beast. The Quest depends on it." He nodded at the Hooded Man. "You stay here and guard him, Elenna!"

"You can count on me and Silver, Tom," said Elenna, sitting on a broken pillar and levelling an arrow at the Hooded Man.

Their enemy only laughed bitterly. "You didn't have the guts to kill me before, girl. Why should I fear you now?"

Elenna's shot was too fast to see. The arrow quivered where it struck, pinning the man's hood to the ground. Flung onto his back, he could only stare up wide-eyed at Silver, who stood over him, baring his teeth in a menacing growl.

"I would not kill an unarmed man," Elenna said, "but my wolf might."

Tom grinned as he watched the Hooded

Man, pale with fright. He knew that Elenna and Silver were just pretending – but their enemy could not be certain of that.

Turning to the wall, he placed a foot firmly on the ladder's bottom rung. "Don't let him go anywhere," he told his friend.

Elenna didn't take her eyes off the Hooded Man. "We won't."

"Now it's time for me to face Vermok," said Tom fiercely, "and finish this – once and for all."

CHAPTER NINE

DUEL ABOVE THE CITY

Don't look down! And don't think about how old this ladder is...

A fierce wind snatched at Tom's clothes as he climbed. The ladder was rusted badly in places. It sagged and wobbled under his weight. Gritting his teeth, Tom pulled himself up hand over hand.

High above him he glimpsed the

menacing shape of Vermok. Tom gritted his teeth and risked a glance over his shoulder. The city was vast, stretching out in every direction towards the hazy horizon. Its limits were marked by a ruined wall. Beyond that were forests and fields as far as Tom could see.

From this height he could see even more of the desolation and destruction: it was as if a giant child had trampled across a toy city. Clouds of dust, stirred by the gusting breeze, obscured whole streets before settling – but up here, the wind was constant and much stronger. It whipped Tom's hair across his eyes, making it hard to see Elenna, Silver and the Hooded Man below. They were tiny now. Off to the west, he could make out two more small figures hurrying towards

the city gates. Ingrid and Edmund, he
guessed. *Thank goodness they'll escape
here unharmed. I hope I'll be able to say
the same for me and Elenna.*

Just as he was thinking this, the
aqueduct shuddered and the ladder
groaned, its brackets tearing away
from the crumbling rock. Tom was

thrown backwards, swaying in mid-air. His fingers lost their grip, and he hung above the ruined city by one hand, the wind shrieking in his ears as his legs dangled.

No! I can't fall to my death now – not when I've come so far!

The ladder creaked as it lurched further back, and Tom felt his grip weakening. He flailed with his other hand, and missed. *My weight will pull it right off the wall...*

My weight...that's it!

Tom fumbled desperately inside his tunic for the token he had won from Linka. Could her single tawny feather help him?

As soon as his fingers grasped it, Tom pushed himself off the ladder. *It's like I'm swimming through air*, he realised. He kicked his legs and turned his body over so that he could push at the ladder. With a metallic shriek, it slammed back against the wall.

Tom gripped the ladder again, his heart pounding with both fear and exhilaration. He heard more buildings collapse in a thunder of stone and dust.

Linka's feather saved me – but I can't stay on this ladder much longer. Tom took a deep steadying breath, gripped a rung with both hands, and began to climb again.

At last he felt the gritty top of the wall under his fingertips. Tom hauled himself up onto it. It was narrow – the deep channel of foul green water was only about two short paces wide – but it felt a lot safer than the rickety ladder. Tom straddled the water, a foot on each side, and faced Vermok, glaring at him from two horse-lengths away.

Drool slavered from the Beast's snarling jaws, and he raked his claws along the stone, tossing his tusks in challenge.

Maybe this was a mistake, thought Tom, risking a glance back over the edge. It was a very long way down,

and the wind still howled and snatched at him. *Vermok doesn't have to reach me with those tusks – he only has to knock me off balance.*

No time to think such thoughts now! Tom raised his shield, the great ruby glowing.

"Vermok!" he shouted fiercely. "You've killed many who walked the Warrior's Road – too many!"

The Beast squealed and tossed his ugly head. As he whipped his one remaining tail, drops of blood scattered. His claws dug great grooves in the crumbling aqueduct, sending shards spinning over the edge.

Tom stood firm, resisting the pull of the vicious wind. "You've met your match this time, Vermok. Your reign of terror is over!"

Snarling, the Spiteful Scavenger coiled

his snake-like tail up over his head.
His muscles stiffened as he crouched,
flanks heaving.

He's trying to trick me, thought Tom.
*He's holding back, waiting for the right
moment to attack – but I'm not sure I can
wait much longer!*

"What's wrong?" Tom shouted.
"Why don't you kill me, too? Are you
afraid of me?"

With a screech of fury, Vermok
charged. Elenna's cry rose up from
below. "Noooooo!"

Tom heard his friend's scream of
warning, but he couldn't spare her
a glance. Bringing his shield to his
side, he steadied himself for Vermok's
attack. The Beast was pounding
towards him, as fast as a gigantic,
galloping horse.

Clenching his jaw, Tom focused on

timing the thundering steps of the Beast. The rhythm was remorseless, and Vermok was almost on him. *Only a few paces more...closer... That's it!*

Sucking in a breath, Tom jumped, and plunged into the deep water beneath him. The shocking cold drove the breath from his lungs, but Tom let the weight of his sword and shield pull him under. Brackish water closed over his head, and his feet touched the bottom of the channel.

Tom ignored the foul taste in his mouth and the clammy touch of weed and algae. Blinking upwards through the green gloom, he saw the pale distorted sunlight blotted out suddenly by a black shape.

Now!

Shoving himself up from the bottom, Tom burst from the stagnant

water, his sword held above him. The
blade struck true, plunging through
Vermok's hide and into his belly.

A terrible squeal ripped the air, and
Tom floundered, staggering to the
edge of the channel.

I've wounded him!

There was black blood on his

hand, dripping thickly down from his sword's blade and hilt. It smelled worse than the water.

As he hauled himself from the channel, covered in green slime and gasping for breath, Tom raised his sword once more. But the Beast was lurching sideways away from him, screaming horribly as his tail lashed in panic and pain. His muscles writhed and his eyes glowed. *He's weakened*, thought Tom, *but he still wants to attack!*

Tom drew back his sword and sprang at the Beast a second time. But before his blade could strike home, Vermok tumbled backwards and crashed to the edge of the aqueduct. With a final shriek, he disappeared over the side.

Tom stumbled forward, wiping

green ooze from his eyes as he kneeled to look over. Not far below, Vermok swung in the howling wind, still flailing. His tail was coiled round a jutting spar of stone. But the Beast was helpless.

The Beast's head twisted towards Tom, eyes glittering with the fury of defeat.

Tom dropped his sword. "You're beaten, Vermok," he shouted. "But a Master never kills a Beast in cold blood."

The giant rat writhed and scrabbled, his claws raking dust and stone fragments that were caught and tossed by the wind. Tom narrowed his eyes against the clouds of blown grit.

Could Vermok manage to climb back even now?

With a thunderous crack, the stone

was ripped away from the wall.
Vermok's tail uncoiled, whipping at
the air as the Beast plummeted to the
ground.

But he never landed. Tom gasped
as Vermok's massive body vanished
in mid-air. All that remained of the
Spiteful Scavenger was a plume of
stone-dust, drifting away on the
gentle breeze.

CHAPTER TEN

THE HOODED MAN REVEALED

The rusted ladder seemed even creakier on the way down – but at least this time, Tom was not climbing towards a deadly Beast. Pain shot through his arms, but at last he saw the solid earth just below him. Breathing a sigh of relief, he jumped down.

Something even paler than the stone-dust gleamed at his feet. Vermok might

have disappeared, but he had left something behind – a single, sickle-shaped ivory tusk.

My next token, Tom thought, bending to pick it up. He slipped it into his pack before trudging back to the others.

With a howl of joy, Silver rushed to greet him. The wolf flinched at the last moment, his muzzle wrinkling, then gave Tom's hand a doubtful lick. Tom rubbed the wolf's mane with one hand as he flicked tendrils of slime from his sleeve.

I obviously don't smell good – even to a wolf!

"Tom!" exclaimed Elenna. She glanced at him, but kept her bow trained on the Hooded Man. "You did it!"

"Yes. It was a hard fight, though," said Tom. He frowned as he saw the flash of a smile from the shadows of his enemy's hood.

"Perhaps I misjudged you, boy," said the Hooded Man, the mysterious grin still playing on his face. "I thought you didn't have it in you. Vermok's been the death of many a pretender, but it seems you're the real thing."

"It seems so," said Tom through gritted teeth. At his side, Silver growled.

"Ah, but there's one Beast you must still face on the Road," said the Hooded Man. "And you'll find this one far more deadly than any you've encountered before. You'll fail at the last hurdle."

Tom had been determined not to rise to his taunts, but the man's sneering tone finally sparked his temper. "You don't know me," he snapped. "So you can keep your words of wisdom."

The Hooded Man threw back his head and roared with laughter.

Elenna frowned at Tom, who clenched his fists with anger. But there was no silencing the Hooded Man, who laughed until his eyes were streaming.

"I don't know you, you say?" Barely able to speak, the Hooded Man wiped his eyes. "You're mistaken. I know you better than anyone – alive or dead!"

Elenna leaped to her feet, her patience exhausted. "Stop talking in riddles!" she shouted. "Explain yourself…" She glanced meaningfully at Silver. "Or I'll remind my wolf how hungry he is!"

"What do you mean?" asked Tom furiously. "How could you possibly know me?"

The Hooded Man's laughter died suddenly. He threw back his hood. His face was so serious, after his uncontrollable laughter, it was unnerving.

"Because," he said, "I *am* you."

Tom felt the ground shift beneath
his feet. This time, he knew, it was
no earthquake. He couldn't avert
his stare from the Hooded Man's
face, and his solemn and determined
blue eyes. Their expression was so
familiar...

Those were the same eyes that
looked back at him when he glanced
into a mountain lake, or when he

eyed his polished sword. The face was older, and scarred…but it was his face. Even the sword was Tom's – just older, with a new and altered hilt.

No wonder the Hooded Man reminded me of my father.

The man gave him a dark smile.

"Why do you think I worked so hard to find you?" he asked. "I came to give you a warning. A warning from yourself! I'm a Tom who knows so much more about this Quest than you do."

"Don't listen to him, Tom," Elenna warned.

But how can I not listen? thought Tom. *This man is me…*

"Beware, younger me," the Hooded Man growled, his eyes glittering. "I've been walking the Warrior's Road for nearly fifty years – and so will you, if you do not heed my warning. The Judge lied to you. The Road is a trick. It never ends."

"Impossible," Tom growled. *After all we've been through – there must be an end. I have to succeed!*

"The choice is yours, Tom," said the Hooded Man. "Accept defeat and go home – or walk this cursed Road forever…and become me!"

Stunned, Tom turned to Elenna.

"What should I do?" he asked. Silver gave a questioning whine, but Elenna seemed speechless as she shook her head.

It's my choice, Tom realised. *Do I pursue my Quest to the end, or do I abandon it? Do I give up on ever being Master of the Beasts again? Do I betray Avantia?*

Tom had conquered five Beasts on

this Quest, had travelled through portals into dangerous new realms. Now, he wasn't even sure if it had been worth it. Doubt flickered in his chest as he gazed out over the ruined city. He was surrounded by chaos. His head felt thick and heavy...

But I have to think. I need to choose my fate!

He looked back at the Hooded Man. His older self was watching him through narrowed eyes.

He's waiting to see what I decide.

Tom turned away. Whatever his path – brave or foolish – it was Tom's decision alone, and he must take the consequences. *While there's blood in my veins*, he told himself, *I will make the right choice.*

Won't I?

Join Tom on the next stage
of the Beast Quest, when he faces

KobA
GHOUL OF THE
SHADOWS!

FREE COLLECTOR CARDS INSIDE!

Series 13: THE WARRIOR'S ROAD
COLLECT THEM ALL!

The Warrior's Road is Tom's toughest challenge
yet. Will he succeed where so many have failed?

SKURIK
THE FOREST DEMON

978 1 40832 402 8

TARGRO
THE ARCTIC MENACE

978 1 40832 403 5

SLIVKA
THE COLD-HEARTED CURSE

978 1 40832 404 2

LINKA
THE SKY CONQUEROR

978 1 40832 405 9

VERMOK
THE SPITEFUL SCAVENGER

978 1 40832 406 6

KOBA
GHOUL OF THE SHADOWS

978 1 40832 407 3

Win an exclusive
Beast Quest T-shirt and goody bag!

In every Beast Quest book the Beast Quest logo is hidden in one of the pictures. Find the logos in books 73 to 78 and make a note of which pages they appear on. Write the six page numbers on a postcard and send it in to us.
Each month we will draw one winner to receive a Beast Quest T-shirt and goody bag.

THE BEAST QUEST COMPETITION:
The Warrior's Road
Orchard Books
338 Euston Road, London NW1 3BH
Australian readers should email:
childrens.books@hachette.com.au

New Zealand readers should write to:
Beast Quest Competition
4 Whetu Place, Mairangi Bay, Auckland, NZ
or email: childrensbooks@hachette.co.nz

Only one entry per child.
Final draw: January 2014

You can also enter this competition
via the Beast Quest website: www.beastquest.co.uk

Join the Quest,
Join the Tribe

www.beastquest.co.uk

Have you checked out the Beast Quest website?
It's the place to go for games, downloads, activities,
sneak previews and lots of fun!

You can read all about your favourite Beasts,
download free screensavers and desktop wallpapers
for your computer, and even challenge your friends
to a Beast Tournament.

Sign up to the newsletter at www.beastquest.co.uk
to receive exclusive extra content and the
opportunity to enter special members-only
competitions. We'll send you up-to-date info on all
the Beast Quest books, including the next exciting
series which features four brand-new Beasts!

Get 30% off all Beast Quest Books at www.beastquest.co.uk
Enter the code BEAST at the checkout.

Offer valid in UK and ROI, offer expires December 2013